# Two Silly Trolls

An I Can Read Book®

# Two Silly Trolls

## by Nancy Jewell
## pictures by Lisa Thiesing

HarperTrophy®

*A Division of* HarperCollins*Publishers*

For Nina -
N. J.

For Katherine -
L. T.

HarperCollins®, ☀®, Harper Trophy®, and I Can Read Book®
are trademarks of HarperCollins Publishers Inc.

Two Silly Trolls
Text copyright © 1992 by Nancy Jewell
Illustrations copyright © 1992 by Lisa Thiesing
Printed in the U.S.A. All rights reserved.
Typography by Daniel C. O'Leary

Library of Congress Cataloging-in-Publication Data
Jewell, Nancy.
  Two silly trolls / by Nancy Jewell ; pictures by Lisa Thiesing.
    p.    cm. —(An I can read book)
  Summary: Nip and Tuck, two troll brothers, share silly experiences,
including building a house without a roof, getting lost on the way to their own
picnic, and sharing a traveling itch.
  ISBN 0-06-022829-6. — ISBN 0-06-022830-X (lib. bdg.)
  ISBN 0-06-444173-3 (pbk.)
  [1. Trolls—Fiction.    2. Brothers—Fiction.]    I. Thiesing, Lisa, ill.
II. Title.    III. Series.
PZ7.J55325Tw    1992                                        90-4387
[E]—dc20                                                        CIP
                                                                AC

First Harper Trophy edition, 1994.

# CONTENTS

# The Goose Bump House

Nip and Tuck lived

under a mushroom.

One day

a bear cub sat down on top of it,

and the mushroom house was no more.

8

The troll brothers

got sticks and stones,

and they built a new house.

"Something hit my nose," said Nip.

"What?" said Tuck.

"I don't know," said Nip.

The trolls looked up.

Raindrops bounced off their foreheads.

Raindrops slid down their cheeks.

Soon they were standing in a puddle.

"We forgot the roof," said Nip.

The trolls made a roof
of leaves and twigs.
They painted the house yellow
with red polka dots.

"Our house has goose bumps,"

said Tuck.

"We will call it

Goose Bump House," said Nip.

So the trolls made a sign

and they moved right in.

# Lost and Found

"Let's go on a picnic
to Shady Tree Pond," said Nip.

"It is too far," said Tuck.

"We will get lost."

"We will not get lost," said Nip.

"I know the way."

The trolls packed a cardboard box
with sandwiches and cookies.
They poured juice into a jug
and set off down the long dirt road.

The road twisted and turned

through the thick woods.

The trolls walked a very long time.

"I am tired," said Tuck.

"Where is that pond?"

"It is just around the bend,"

said Nip.

"How do you know?" asked Tuck.

"See all the trees?" said Nip.

"There are lots of trees

at Shady Tree Pond."

18

The trolls walked and walked,

but they did not come to a pond.

"I am thirsty," said Tuck.

"Are we almost there?"

"Yes," said Nip.

"How can you tell?" asked Tuck.

"Listen to the birds," said Nip.

"There are lots of birds
at Shady Tree Pond."

The trolls walked and walked,

but they did not come to a pond.

Tuck sat down on the ground
and ate half a sandwich.
Nip ate the other half.
"I think we are lost,"
said Tuck.
"No!" said Nip.
"I know the way."

The trolls drank some juice

and walked some more.

They ate some cookies

and walked some more.

But they still did not come to a pond.

"Stop!" cried Nip.

"I have seen that tree before."

"And I have seen that bush before,"

said Tuck.

"We are at the pond!"

cried Nip.

The trolls raced down the path.

They ran past the tree,

and they ran past the bush.

Then they stopped

and looked at each other.

"That is a funny-looking pond,"

said Tuck.

"It looks like our house,"

said Nip.

"It *is* our house," said Tuck.

"You see!" said Nip.

"We are *not* lost."

"We are not?" said Tuck.

26

"Of course not," said Nip.

"We are home."

So the trolls had a picnic

in their own backyard,

and they fed the crumbs

to the birds.

# The Itch

"I can't sleep," said Tuck.

"Why?" said Nip.

"My foot itches," said Tuck.

"Why don't you scratch it?"

said Nip.

"That is a good idea," said Tuck.

"Good night, Nip."

"Good night, Tuck."

"My other foot itches,"

said Tuck a minute later.

"Scratch it," said Nip.

"I did," said Tuck.

"The more I scratch,

the more I itch."

"Then stop scratching," said Nip.

Tuck lay very still.

His feet itched and itched.

"It is hard not to scratch,"

said Tuck.

"Think about your knees," said Nip.

"Why?" said Tuck.

"Then you will not think
about your feet,"
said Nip.

Tuck turned over on his left side.

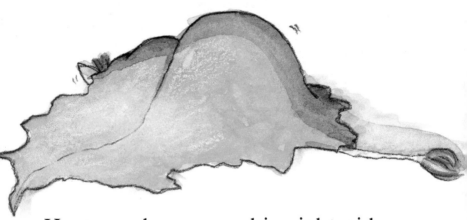

He turned over on his right side.

He sat up in bed.

"Now what is the matter?" said Nip.

"My knees itch," said Tuck.

"Think about arms," said Nip.

Tuck thought about arms.

The itch jumped to his arms.

He thought about chins.

It jumped to his chin.

"This itch does not go away,"

said Tuck. "It just moves!"

"Yes," said Nip.

"It is a traveling itch."

Suddenly Nip's foot began to itch.

Then his other foot itched,

then his knees,

and his arms,

and his chin.

Soon both trolls

were itching and scratching,

scratching and itching.

When the sun came up,

they yawned and got out of bed.

"You stopped scratching," said Tuck.

"So did you," said Nip.

"Where are our itches?" said Tuck.

"Those itches must have traveled
somewhere else," said Nip.

The trolls yawned again
and went to get breakfast.

# The Cookie

"I want a cookie," said Tuck.

"What kind?" asked Nip.

"Chocolate chip," said Tuck.

"With big, fat chips."

"And nuts," said Nip.

"I don't like nuts," said Tuck.

"And raisins," said Nip.

"I don't want raisins," said Tuck.

"Nuts and raisins and peanut butter,"

said Nip.

"No!" said Tuck.

"And whipped cream," said Nip.

41

"That is an Everything Cookie,"
said Tuck.

"That is the best kind," said Nip.

"But I want a chocolate-chip cookie,"
said Tuck.

"I want a chocolate-chip-nut-raisin-
peanut-butter-whipped-cream cookie,"
said Nip.

But there was only one cookie

in the cookie jar.

It was a plain vanilla wafer.

"This is a Nothing Cookie,"

said Tuck.

He took a bite.

Then Nip took a bite.

"This cookie is good," said Tuck.

"This cookie is very good," said Nip.

# The Sweater

Tuck loved his green wool sweater.

It was soft and baggy

and had two big pockets.

He wore it all the time,

even to bed.

"Tuck," said Nip,

"your sweater is ugly."

"It is not ugly," said Tuck.

"It is just old."

"It has stains," said Nip.

"Those are not stains," said Tuck.

"The red spot is ketchup,

and the yellow spot is mustard."

48

"Your sweater has holes," said Nip.

"You cannot see them," said Tuck.

"I have put Band-Aids on the holes."

"I cannot take walks

with you anymore," said Nip.

"The other trolls laugh at us."

50

So Tuck gave his sweater

to a mouse for her nest.

Then the trolls went to town

to buy Tuck a new sweater.

The store had lots of sweaters.

Red sweaters and blue sweaters,

pink sweaters and purple sweaters.

Tuck tried on only one.

He paid for his sweater,

and the trolls started home.

"Why don't you put on
your new sweater?"
asked Nip.

"Because it does not feel
like my old sweater," said Tuck.

"It is just like your old sweater,"
said Nip.

"It is not," said Tuck.

"My old sweater was soft and baggy.

This sweater feels

scratchy and stiff."

55

The new sweater sat in its box
for the rest of the day.
Tuck did not wear it
for his evening walk
or when he went to bed.

"Put on your new sweater,"
said Nip.

"You know you cannot sleep
without it."

"I cannot sleep

without my *old* sweater,"

said Tuck.

"But it is the same sweater,"

said Nip.

"It is *not* the same," said Tuck.

"I do not *know* this sweater!"

"I am sorry I made you give away

your old sweater," said Nip.

"That is all right," said Tuck,

but he could not fall asleep.

Neither could Nip.

Nip got up

and went to the closet.

He got out the new sweater.

He pulled it and yanked it.

60

He jumped up and down on it.

Then he got ketchup and mustard,

scissors and Band-Aids.

"Here," said Nip.

"I have fixed up your new sweater."

"It is just like my old sweater,"

said Tuck.

And he put it on.

Tuck wore the new-old sweater

the rest of the night.

He wore it the next day,

and he wore it the next night.

Tuck wore his sweater all the time,

even to bed.